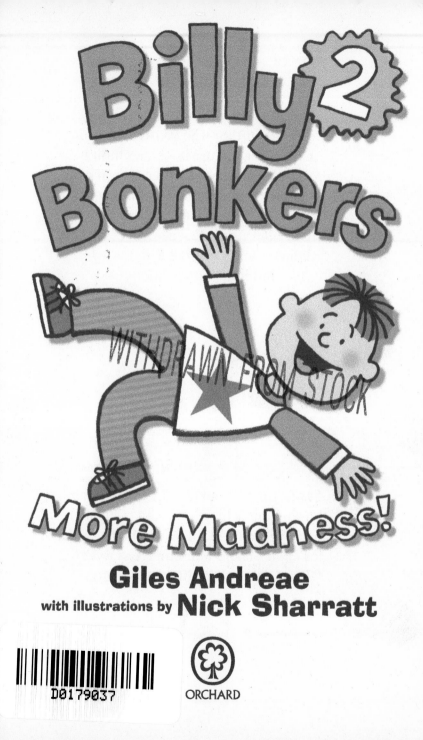

Billy 2 Bonkers

More Madness!

Giles Andreae

with illustrations by **Nick Sharratt**

ORCHARD

Giles Andreae is an award-winning
children's author who has written many
bestselling picture books, including
Giraffes Can't Dance and *Commotion in the Ocean*.
He is probably most famous as the creator of
the phenomenally successful Purple Ronnie,
Britain's favourite stickman. Giles lives in
London and Cornwall with his wife
and four young children.

Nick Sharratt studied art at
St Martin's School of Art and has been
drawing for as long as he can remember.
He has written and illustrated many books
for children and won numerous awards
for his work. Nick lives in Brighton.

Contents

Billy Bonkers

and the
Great Sports Day Fiasco

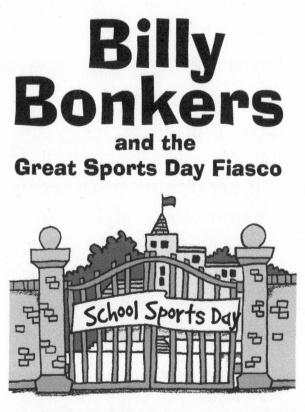

Sports Day at Billy and Betty Bonkers' school was always an interesting occasion.

Every year, the children's events were a testament to teamwork, good grace, manners and sportsmanship, with only the occasional tearful loser at the lower end of the school. But the parents' events...

...the parents' events were little short of WAR. And no event was more hotly contested than the Fathers' Race.

On the morning of the event, Billy bounced downstairs for his usual bowl or three of porridge to be greeted by his very chirpy-looking, very relaxed father. This was unusual, as Mr Bonkers was normally completely unable to sleep for nights before Sports Day, due to his nerves.

The Great Sports Day Fiasco

"Morning, Billy," said Mr Bonkers, still in his pyjamas. "And what a super one it is, don't you think?"

"Are you all right?" asked Billy, surprised.

"All right?" said Mr Bonkers. "Never been better!"

"Did you sleep OK?"

"Like a baby!" replied Mr Bonkers.

"He did!" came a voice from upstairs. It was Mrs Bonkers. "Unbelievable! First time in years. Something must be wrong! Now, are you sure you want these baggy old trousers for today, Sausage? You haven't worn them for ages.

What about those horrid shiny shorts you normally wear for Sports Day?" Mrs Bonkers was rummaging through the mountain of laundry in her ironing pile.

"Yes, your 'go-faster shorts', Dad," smirked Betty, Billy's older sister. "The world's most embarrassing legwear."

"Good lord," said Mr Bonkers, looking up from his newspaper. "Have you seen this? A pair of cheetahs has escaped from the wildlife park! Cheetahs...roaming around endangering the public. How can they let that happen? It's mad! The world's gone mad!"

"Never mind about that now, Sausage," said Mrs Bonkers, coming down the stairs.

"You just get yourself ready. Here are your trousers. Billy and Betty, could you help me with the picnic, please?"

"Um, actually, Piglet, do you mind if Billy comes with me for a moment?" said Mr Bonkers, putting down his paper and springing to his feet. "There's just something in the shed I'd like him to help me with."

Billy Bonkers

Mr Bonkers grabbed his trousers and took Billy outside into the garden. Billy loved going into his father's shed. Mr Bonkers enjoyed tinkering with machines at the weekends and, over the years, he had come up with all sorts of peculiar labour-saving inventions, most of which in fact caused a great deal more labour than they saved, but, as Mrs Bonkers always said, it kept him out of trouble, and anything that kept him out of trouble was worth more than the trouble that it caused.

"Hello, Nigel!" shouted Mr Rocket, the Bonkers' neighbour, from over the fence. He was performing some elaborate stretching exercises in his garden.

"Morning, Roger! I see you've got new trainers."

"Limited edition," said Mr Rocket. "Airsprung, fully-cushioned, high-performance,

supalite, all-surface, speed-tech trainers, actually. I'm going to win the race again this year and nothing's going to stop me."

"I wouldn't be so sure," said Mr Bonkers, with a twinkle in his eye. "Come on, Billy – to the shed."

* * *

Billy Bonkers

"Ta-daaah!" trumpeted Mr Bonkers, whisking an old curtain off a pile of rusty metal rods that were bolted together around an equally ancient-looking motor.

"Um…what is it?" asked Billy.

"What is it?" snorted Mr Bonkers. "It's only my brand-new, custom-made, seventy-miles-an-hour BIONIC LEGS!"

"Bionic legs?" said Billy. "What are they?"

"Look," said Mr Bonkers, taking off his pyjamas and stepping into the strange machine. "I took the lawn mower apart – every single bit of it – and then I made these leg braces out of the handle..." He strapped the rods around his thighs. "The motor sits between them, inside my underpants, and *vroooooooom*! Your dad wins the Fathers' Race!"

"Isn't that cheating?" asked Billy.

"Cheating's only cheating if you're found out," said Mr Bonkers. "And that's where these baggy old trousers come in. See?" he said, slipping them on. "Completely invisible! But that's not even the clever bit. Here, take a look at this."

Mr Bonkers handed Billy a small black box.

"The remote control from your old car," he said. "I jigged it around a bit and, hey presto, the bionic leg controller! Just ram the throttle lever here up to max and you will be able to steer the legs – and me – to victory!"

"But, Dad…" began Billy.

"Never mind 'but, Dad,' son! We're going to win the race! My name will be on the cup! Roger Rocket's going down! Oh, sweet, sweet victory!"

"Come on, boys!" shouted Mrs Bonkers, her arms piled high with picnic baskets, cool boxes, Tupperware, Thermos flasks, rugs and cushions. "Let's go or we'll be late!"

The Great Sports Day Fiasco

So Mr and Mrs Bonkers, Billy and Betty piled into the car, and it wasn't long before they were settled beside the athletics track of Billy and Betty's school, enjoying one of Mrs Bonkers' famous home-made pork pies.

* * *

After lunch, and after several events in which Billy and Betty had both been beaten by Rollo Rocket, who was perhaps even more competitive than his father, the headmaster's voice rang through the loudspeaker system again.
"Now, ladies and gentlemen," he announced, **"it's time for the Fathers' Race.**

Billy Bonkers

And, gentlemen, please remember that this race is only meant to be a bit of fun. We don't want any more accidents like last year. The hospital cannot cope."

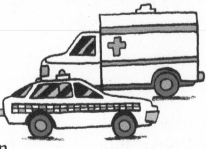

There was an ambulance waiting by the side of the track and several policemen had been drafted in, in case of emergency.

"Right, Billy," said Mr Bonkers. "The time has come. Have you got the remote?" he whispered.

"Yes, Dad," Billy whispered back, "but I do think…"

"Then let's go!" said Mr Bonkers, walking in really quite a peculiar way towards the start line.

All the fathers lined up together.

"Start the motor," whispered Mr Bonkers to Billy.

"How?" asked Billy.

"The ripcord sticking out of my waistband. Pull it hard."

Billy pulled, but nothing happened.

"OK," said Mr Bonkers. "It needs a bit of choke."

He fiddled around inside his trouser pockets, trying not to attract the attention of any of the other dads.

"Again!" whispered Mr Bonkers, urgently.

This time, Billy pulled and a faint *putt...putt...putt* came from the trousers. Then nothing.

"Are you all right, Sausage?" said Mrs Bonkers, who had come to watch the race from the sideline with all the other mums.

"Oh, um, yes...probably just a bit of indigestion," Mr Bonkers replied.

"On your marks..." said the headmaster.

Billy pulled the ripcord again. "Come on, Billy," whispered Mr Bonkers. "Harder!"

"Get set..." said the headmaster. The other fathers were all crouching now, their fingers poised on the grass of the track and their eyes narrowed towards the finishing line.

BANG! The starter gun fired and all the fathers sprang to their feet. All the fathers, that is, except for Mr Bonkers.

"Come on, Billy," he shouted, "put some muscle into it!"

Billy yanked the ripcord as hard as he could, fell over backwards, and with a

Vrooooooooom!

the motor roared into life.

"Good lord!" said Candy Rocket, Roger's wife, to Mrs Bonkers. "What have you been feeding him?"

But before Mrs Bonkers could answer, her husband shot past her like a tornado.

he shouted.

Billy did as he was told and pushed the throttle lever on the remote control up to maximum.

He was some way behind all the other dads but, quickly, Mr Bonkers began to catch up.

Many of the fathers were already rolling around on the track clutching various parts of their anatomies, due to the usual round of tripping and barging from the other competitors. Mr Bonkers found it hard to steer past these casualties because, well, it was Billy who was doing the steering and it

took a bit of getting used to. But it wasn't long before he (and, of course, Billy) had manoeuvred his way towards the front of the race.

Billy Bonkers

"Come on, Dad!" shrieked Betty. "You're going to do it! Come on! COME ON!"

Then, with another thrust on the remote's throttle from Billy, there was a sudden **whooooooooosh!** and Mr Bonkers screeched ahead of the pack. He reached the finishing line a good twenty metres ahead of any of the other dads, breaking the tape (and, in fact, the record for the Fathers' Race) with the biggest smile on his face that Mrs Bonkers had ever seen.

"That's my Sausage!" shouted Mrs Bonkers, astonished. "He's done it! He's finally done it! Oh, he'll be so proud."

"Yes," said Candy Rocket. "And if he's anything like my Roger, you'll never hear the end of it. He'll be a nightmare to live with from this  day forward. By the way, shouldn't he have stopped by now?"

Mrs Bonkers looked at her husband. He certainly seemed to be milking his lap of honour.

"You can stop now, Sausage," she shouted. "You've won! Well done! You don't need to carry on running. Um, everyone knows that you're the winner..."

But Mr Bonkers was not going to stop. You see, in his eagerness to get his bionic legs to go as fast as they possibly could, Mr Bonkers had completely forgotten to put a stop button on the remote control. And Billy had rammed the throttle up to full speed so hard that it was now well and truly stuck.

shouted Billy. "It's jammed! The throttle's jammed! I can't get it off maximum!"

"What's he doing?" shrieked Candy Rocket. "He's heading straight towards the picnics. Is he hungry or something? I've never seen a man run that fast before…not even for food!"

Help!

Billy tried desperately to steer his dad back towards the athletics track but, by now, Mr Bonkers was too far out of range for the remote control to have any effect whatsoever.

Then... SPLAT! Mr Bonkers sprinted right into a huge chocolate cake that was laid out on the Rockets' picnic rug for tea. CRASH! He hit the next picnic, and plates and cups went spinning in every direction. SQUELCH! He bounded through a dish full of sausages, sandwiches and scotch eggs. Food was flying everywhere.

Then finally... SMASH! Mr Bonkers charged straight into the table where the headmaster was carefully setting out the various cups, medals and prizes that he was going to present later that afternoon.

"You lunatic!" yelled the headmaster, as he fell flat on his face amongst the silverware. "S...T...O...P!"

"I can't!" shouted Mr Bonkers over his shoulder. "S...O...R...R...Y!"

Then something extraordinary happened. In front of the whole school, Mr Bonkers, who was now running faster than ever,

ran straight through the hedge at the edge of the school grounds,

The Great Sports Day Fiasco

sprinted through
the fruit farm
next door,

crashed through
a wooden fence,
and found himself charging at top speed
the wrong way down a six-lane motorway
with exhaust fumes spewing out of his
trousers, and squashed tomatoes, plums and
gooseberries splattered
all over his face.

Yes, you could safely say that Mr Bonkers' plan had not gone, well, according to plan.

Meanwhile, back at school, there was pandemonium. Nobody knew what to do – least of all Billy, who was left clutching the now useless remote control.

Betty rushed to his side. "What's that you were saying just now?" she asked. "About a throttle or something?"

Billy knew that he had to come clean if they were to have any chance of rescuing their dad, so he explained everything.

"…but now the throttle's jammed and the steering control's out of range!" he finished. "It's completely useless!"

The Great Sports Day Fiasco

"Well then, we'll just have to get it back in range," replied Betty. "Come on! I think I might have an idea."

Betty ran over to one of the policemen at the side of the track. "Quick!" she shouted. "My dad's wearing some bionic legs that are going at full speed the wrong way down the motorway and we've got to stop him. My brother's got the remote control, only it's stuck and…oh, never mind, just get into your car and drive!"

The policeman was so astonished that he did exactly what Betty told him. He even drove onto the motorway the wrong way which, I can tell you for free, is a very unusual thing for a policeman to do indeed.

"Look! There he is!" shouted Betty over the wail of the police car's siren, as they swerved and skidded to avoid the other dumbfounded drivers who were hurtling towards them on the road.

"He's running at seventy miles an hour!" yelled the policeman. "That's impossible! This is crazy! CRAZY!"

"See if the control works, Billy," shouted Betty. "Try the steering. We may be close enough now."

Billy did as he was told and, to his astonishment, his dad started veering sideways – first to the left, and then to the right – just as Billy moved the steering lever on his control.

"It's working!" shouted Billy. "He's in range!"

But Mr Bonkers was now running so fast that just a twitch on the remote altered his direction so dramatically that it was all Billy could do to avoid steering his dad right under the wheels of any number of terrified drivers as they whizzed and screeched past him, their mouths hanging open in disbelief.

"Right," said Betty. "Move him over to the side of the road. He should be safer there."

"Throw a net over him!" shouted the policeman. "That'll stop him. There's one there in the back."

"Throw a net over him?" shouted Betty. "Are you mad? It's terribly dangerous, and besides…"

But she never finished this sentence because, in the woods along the side of the motorway, she suddenly caught sight of two flashes of yellow and black fur running beside them as fast as…well, as fast as only a cheetah could possibly run.

"It's them!" she said excitedly. "The cheetahs from the wildlife park that Dad was reading about this morning. We've got to stop them. They're a danger to the public!"

"Danger to the public?" shouted Billy. "What do you think Dad is if not a danger to the public? And he's our dad, too! Let's stop him first...please!

"Quite right," said the policeman. "And anyway, how would we get to the cheetahs? You can't drive a car into the woods – particularly not at seventy miles an hour!"

"Hang on," said Betty, grabbing the net from the floor of the car. "I think I might have an idea. Billy, if we get close enough to Dad, you can climb out of the window, jump onto his shoulders with your remote control and steer him towards the cheetahs. When you get close enough, just throw this net over them and *voilà*! Two captured cheetahs and Dad safely off the road."

"But how do I stop Dad?" asked Billy. "Betty, are you completely mad?"

"I'm sure you'll think of something," smiled Betty. "Now, come on, we've no time to lose!"

So the policeman steered the car to the side of the road, still driving very fast indeed, and Billy carefully edged out of the window.

I must tell you now that even taking off your seat belt in the back of a moving car, let alone climbing out of the window of one travelling quite as fast as that particular police car, is a very dangerous thing to do indeed. It is something you must never do in any circumstances whatsoever – not even if your dad is running the wrong way down the motorway at seventy miles an hour in a pair of bionic legs.

Anyway, where was I? Oh, yes. So, Billy climbed slowly out of the window and, with the scariest jump of his life, he launched himself out of the car and - **BUMP!** - landed right on top of his dad's shoulders!

"I've made it!" he shouted. "Right, Dad, into the woods! Let's go!"

Holding tightly onto the net and the remote control, Billy gradually steered his dad towards the woods.

"Wait!" shouted Mr Bonkers, who was panting and wheezing like a madman. "I can't go into those woods. Look, there's barbed wire all the way along the side!"

"We've got to," yelled Billy. "Just jump. It's the only way we're going to catch the cheetahs!"

"Catch cheetahs?" shrieked Mr Bonkers. "Billy, are you out of your mind?"

"Oh, um, sorry Dad," said Billy. "I guess you didn't know." Then he gulped and pushed the steering lever to the left, and Mr Bonkers, whose face was already puce and pouring with sweat, nearly exploded.

"NO!" shrieked Mr Bonkers, as Billy steered him straight towards the woods.

"JUMP!" yelled Billy.

"Ouuuuuwww!" screamed Mr Bonkers as his trousers snagged on the top of the barbed wire, and were ripped clean off.

The Great Sports Day Fiasco

Mr Bonkers was now pounding through the woods in just a pair of old underpants, which were billowing exhaust, his bionic legs finally fully exposed for all the world to see.

You could say that this had not been a good day for him, and it was not over yet.

Suddenly, Billy saw the cheetahs.

"HELP!" screamed Mr Bonkers. "Wild animals!" He tried desperately to run in the opposite direction but, of course, Billy had the remote, so Billy was in control.

"Sorry, Dad," he managed to shout. "But it's for our own good."

Carefully, Billy steered Mr Bonkers right up behind the cheetahs. I cannot read the thoughts of cheetahs (or any other animals, for that matter), but I think I could safely say that these cheetahs were very surprised indeed to see a boy riding on the shoulders of a man with metal legs and smoking underpants who was running along at seventy miles an hour behind them.

Then Billy had an idea. He grabbed at the branch of a passing tree, snapped it off and, with all his might, jammed it right into the blur of his father's still-pounding bionic legs.

Instantly, Mr Bonkers tripped and went flying to the ground. Billy was launched off his shoulders.

He just had time to hold out the net and drop it over the cheetahs...

...before he too landed flat on his bum in a very prickly bramble bush indeed.

But he didn't mind. He had finally managed to bring his dad to a halt and, more than that, he had actually caught the cheetahs!

"You've done it!" shouted Betty. "Billy, you're a hero!"

"Yes, indeed, young man," said the policeman, as he too caught up with what had happened. "You're a hero, and a very brave one at that. Congratulations! Now, let's all jump back in the car. I'm sure your mother will want to know what you've been up to."

* * *

"Lordy lorks, you're safe!" gasped Mrs Bonkers, running towards them as they climbed out of the police car. "Billy, Betty, you're SAFE!

"And YOU," she said to her husband. "What on earth have you been up to?"

As she looked down at the now twisted metal rods around his legs and the lawn mower motor still strapped inside his underpants, Mrs Bonkers couldn't help but smile.

"You men," she said. "You're all the same. Win, win, win. That's all it's about for you, isn't it? Now, come on, back home and into the bath, the lot of you. Look, you're filthy!"

Back at home, Billy, Betty and Mr Bonkers explained everything.

"So where's the remote control now?" asked Mrs Bonkers.

"Here," said Billy.

"Does it work?" she said.

"Yes," replied Billy.

"Well, kind of."

"I think I'll have that, then," said Mrs Bonkers. "It could come in very useful later. There's no end of chores around the house that I'd like your father to do!"

Then she took something out of her pocket and hung it around Mr Bonkers' neck. It was the gold medal from the Fathers' Race. "I kept it for you," she said, putting her arms around him and giving him a hug. "I thought you'd like it."

Mr Bonkers closed his eyes and grinned from ear to ear. "Thank you, Piglet," he said. "Thank you."

THE END

Billy Bonkers

and the
Miracle at Loch Ness

Mr Bonkers had decided to take his family to Scotland – to Loch Ness, in fact – for this year's summer holiday.

Nobody quite knew why. For *her* holiday, Mrs Bonkers had wanted a break from the housework, but they were staying in a self-catering cottage.

Betty had wanted to get a suntan, but it was raining. Billy had wanted to go on a rollercoaster, but there was no such thing for miles around. But Mr Bonkers...Mr Bonkers thought it was an ideal place because the local scenery would make a terrific subject on which to try out his new video camera.

"Oh yes," said Mr Bonkers in the car on their way up north, "the Luminax 550i widescreen megapixel image-stabilising digicam. Quite a baby, this one!" He carefully repacked every little wire and accessory back into the box it had come in for the umpteenth time. "It's got a thirty-six times optical zoom, don't you know!"

"Yes, Dad, we do know," said Betty. "You've told us a hundred times before."

"Look, here it is!" announced Mr Bonkers, as they finally made it to the house. "1 Nessie Cottages. They do have a sense of humour, these Scots."

"You mean you don't believe in the Loch Ness Monster?" said Mrs Bonkers, smiling wryly. "Well, why have you dragged us all the way up here for our holiday, then?"

"The Loch Ness Monster!" snorted Mr Bonkers, as they unpacked the car. "Nonsense, piffle, balderdash and bunk! Nessie's just a ploy dreamt up by the locals to bring more tourist money into the area."

"Well, do remember to charge up your Luminax 550 whatchamacallit anyway," said Mrs Bonkers. "You never know!"

"What kind of an idiot would forget to do that?" replied her husband. "Honestly, Piglet! Now, is supper ready? I'm starving."

* * *

"It's raining again," said Betty as she, Billy and Mr and Mrs Bonkers drove down to the loch the following day.

"Yes, we can see that, thank you," said Mrs Bonkers, pulling into the car park. "Now, come on, everybody, out into the, um, nice fresh air."

"But it's freezing," moaned Billy, "and there's nothing to do."

"Never mind," said Mrs Bonkers, breezily. "Let's make the best of it. Why don't you try a bit of fishing. Sausage," she said to her husband, "will you get Billy's rod from the car?"

"Oh, blast," said Mr Bonkers. "Knew I'd forget something. But I think there's a spare reel in the glove box. We can stick a twig through the hole in the middle and roll up some bread for bait."

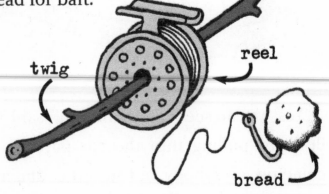

twig

reel

bread

"I can't get this line out into the water without a rod," said Billy, standing at the edge of the loch. "And I don't want to wade in and get my trainers wet."

"Never mind, I'm sure Dad will lend you his new wellies," said Mrs Bonkers. "Won't you, Nigel?"

When his wife called him by his real name, Mr Bonkers knew better than to do anything except exactly what he was told.

"Oh, um, yes, of course, Piglet," said Mr Bonkers. "I don't mind having cold, squelchy toes. Don't mind at all."

So he handed his boots to Billy, and Billy waded out into the water with his fishing line.

Almost immediately, Billy felt a tug.

"Woah!" he shouted. "This is a big one. No, it's not…it's a *huge* one!"

His line was spinning out so fast that the reel hummed and whirred on the little twig that Billy was holding. Then it stopped, and suddenly Billy saw flashes of silver and green just beneath the surface, not far away.

Oh crikey, it's mammoth!

he yelled.

Betty, Mum, Dad! Look!

Betty and Mrs Bonkers came running, but Mr Bonkers was busy studying a

Tourist Information board at the edge of the car park.

"Ancient legend," he mumbled, chewing on a sandwich. "Twenty sightings a year…hokum, I say. Nonsense, piffle, balderdash and bunk!"

Billy's reel began spinning again. Then it went slack again.

"It's coming towards us," shouted Betty. "Look! You can see the colour of its back… just there. *What a fish!* WHAT A FI—!"

But she never got to finish because suddenly, right in front of the astonished faces of Billy and Betty and Mrs Bonkers, the fish broke the surface of the water. Only it wasn't a fish. As I think you may have already guessed, it was none other than…

THE LOCH NESS MONSTER!

I don't know if *you've* ever been lucky enough to see the Loch Ness Monster, or any monster at all for that matter, but there was no doubt that Billy was staring straight into the eyes of something that looked like it had come right out of the pages of a storybook.

And, what's more, *it* was staring straight back at him.

The Miracle at Loch Ness

It had huge dark eyes, enormous jaws with rows and rows of sharp teeth, smooth blue-ish grey skin and a bright silver-green stripe all the way down its long, long neck.

"Sausage!" yelled Mrs Bonkers. "Get your camera! Quick!"

"What's that?" said Mr Bonkers, still studying the notice board.

"Oh, blast. You've made me drop my sandwich."

He picked it up, carefully brushed off the mud, and began eating again.

"Dad!" shouted Betty. "Quick!"

"What is it?" barked Mr Bonkers. "You know, the rubbish it says here about the monster is really taking it too far. I mean, do they think we're idiots or something?"

"DAD!" yelled Betty again. "The monster!"

Mr Bonkers turned round, screamed, and dropped his sandwich again.

Monster!

he yelled.

Monster! MONSTER!

Now, the Loch Ness Monster, as you may know, is famously shy, so when it witnessed all this commotion, it took one more look at Billy, then turned and swam away at full speed, its head still arched above the surface of the water and Billy's fishing line, of course, still in its mouth.

The monster took more and more line as it bolted away. But there was only so much line on the reel that Billy was holding and, as you might expect with a monster swimming as fast as the Loch Ness Monster now was, it very soon came to the end.

I don't know if you've ever been brave enough to tie a wobbly tooth to an open door with a piece of cotton. I certainly haven't. But, if you have, you will know that, as you swing the door closed, the piece of cotton is pulled tight and –

SPROING! – it yanks your tooth out quickly and, I am told, relatively painlessly.

Well, this is exactly what happened to Billy. As the reel in his hand came to an end, the fishing line was pulled tight and – SPROING! – like a loose tooth on the end of a piece of cotton, Billy was catapulted high up into the air.

He turned and twisted and tumbled through the sky until – **SLAM!** – Billy hit the water at, well, at a very high speed indeed.

And because the Loch Ness Monster, and therefore Billy, was going so fast, Billy didn't fall *down* into the water at all. He hit the surface feet first, still wearing his dad's wellies, and found that he was, in fact, standing up! The giant wellies were acting just like waterskis. Yes, Billy found himself actually waterskiing behind the Loch Ness Monster!

"Quick, Dad!" yelled Betty. "Take some video! This is incredible!"

"Excellent idea!" said Mr Bonkers, fumbling excitedly in his bag. He pulled out his camera and pointed it at Billy, who was now swerving and carving behind the monster in really quite a graceful manner.

"It's not working," shouted Mr Bonkers. "Everything's black. It must be broken!"

"Did you remember to charge it up?" asked Betty.

"Oh blast,"  muttered Mr Bonkers under his breath. "Blast, blast, BLAST!"

"Never mind the silly camera!" shrieked Mrs Bonkers. "Billy's in terrible danger!

Lordy lorks, our only son is about to get eaten by an enormous prehistoric monster and all you two can do is worry about a wretched camera! Look…he's not even wearing a life jacket!"

"Hang on a minute," said Betty. "I think I might have an idea! Dad, you can use your phone!"

"Use my phone?" said Mr Bonkers. "Are you out of your mind, girl? Why would I want to make a phone call at a time like this?"

"Not to make a phone call, Dad," continued Betty. "To take some video! Your phone is bound to have a camera on it. Every phone does nowadays."

"A camera…on a telephone?" exclaimed Mr Bonkers. "She's mad! The girl's gone mad! Nutty as nougat. Loopy as a fruit cake!"

"Look, Dad, just give me your phone," said Betty.

Mr Bonkers did as he was told and, after a few quick presses on the buttons, Betty pointed the phone at Billy.

"It's working!" she said. "Wow! Look at that!"

On the tiny screen of his phone, Mr Bonkers could actually see Billy flying along in broad daylight behind the Loch Ness Monster! And, as Betty continued to film them, the monster began to twist and turn and Billy carved, slalomed and jumped behind it through the reeds and all the way along the loch.

"Wicked!" yelled Billy as he zoomed past his family with the biggest smile on his face that Betty had ever seen.

This is A...M...A...Z...I...N...G!

"Incredible!" yelled Mr Bonkers, leaping up and down with excitement. "This film will make us a fortune! Of course, I knew exactly how to do that camera thing...you know...with the phone and stuff."

"Here, Betty, give it to me," he continued. "Let's have a look at it. Let's see what... Oooooh...wooooaaaaah..."

In his haste to grab the phone from Betty, it slipped out of his hands. He juggled with it, trying desperately to catch it, but the phone slipped from his grasp again and fell with a **PLOP!** into the water.

"Oh no!" yelled Mr Bonkers. "It's ruined! Betty, whatever do we do now?"

Just then, a large tour bus pulled into the car park behind them.

Mr Bonkers looked up with delight. "Hallelujah!" he shouted. "Foreign tourists! That coach will be like a mobile electronics shop!"

For once in his life, Mr Bonkers was actually right. As the visitors began to disembark from the bus, it quickly became clear that there wasn't a single one of them who didn't have a camera of one sort or another dangling around his (or her) neck. Many had several.

Mr Bonkers ran into the middle of them.

"Hello! Please! Thank you! Lovely day! Camera! Camera borrow?" he stammered, pointing and then pulling at the camera of one of the bemused tourists.

The man looked at Mr Bonkers with an expression of alarm.

"These Brits are crazy," explained his wife in a heavy American accent. "Better give it to the man."

He held out his camera to Mr Bonkers

with a sympathetic smile, as though offering food to a wild animal.

Mr Bonkers grabbed the camera, ran back to the edge of the loch and quickly began filming. Billy and the monster were still flying through the water, a big smile on *both* of their faces. The monster seemed to be enjoying this as much as Billy.

But, as soon as Mr Bonkers pointed the camera at Nessie and began filming, the monster took one look and dived down below the surface of the water.

Suddenly, there was a clamour behind Mr Bonkers.

"Look! Look!" the tourists were shouting. They had now made their way to the edge of the loch. "That boy's flyin' across the water! There's no boat, no rope, no nuthin'! The boy's magic! He's a marvel! He's...a MIRACLE!"

The sound of shutters clicking and cameras whirring filled the air as they all jostled to take photographs and videos of the first boy ever to skim across the water entirely under his own power.

You see, Nessie was now so deep below the surface that, from the shore, there was no sign of the monster at all. And fishing line, which Billy was clinging onto, is, as I'm sure you know, practically invisible. So it did seem to everybody as though Billy was zooming across the surface of the water without any method of propulsion at all but his own mysterious energy.

It wasn't long before the local newspaper and TV people arrived, shortly followed by national – and then international – news crews.

The monster swam one last circle around the loch and, as they approached the shore where the assembled crowd had gathered, Billy looked down into the water and was

sure he could see
a large, dark eye
wink at him as
Nessie's face lit
up one last
time in a smile.

Billy carved across
the loch, dropped the reel into the water
and skied right up onto the shore.

"Miracle boy! Miracle boy!"
everyone was
shouting.
The tourists
were now
falling over
themselves
to have their
photographs
taken with this
new child sensation.

Even the local mayor had arrived and he quickly marched over to Billy with a huge smile on his face.

"Well, m'lad," he began. "Seems like you're our new attraction! What a *thing* that is that you're able to do! Unbelievable!"

"Well, it wasn't really me," replied Billy. "It was the monster. You see, I was skiing behind the monster – behind Nessie!"

"Oh ho ho!" laughed the mayor. "Now, don't you try to pull that one on me! That Nessie myth's just a load of old hokum

77

that my predecessors dreamt up to attract more tourist money to the area! Nessie indeed! No such thing! Ho ho ho…ho ho ho ho!"

The mayor seemed truly tickled by Billy's story and Billy did indeed start to think that the whole thing sounded a little far-fetched.

"Well," continued the mayor, "we've no need for any more myths now. We've got the real thing! *The loch where the miracle boy flew across the water.* That'll bring no end of tourists here. We'll all be rich! You deserve a reward. What can we possibly give you to say thank you?"

Billy thought for a moment. "Well, we are in Scotland," he said. "And I *am* rather fond of porridge."

"Porridge it will be, then," announced the mayor. "Lorry loads of it!"

Billy was very happy indeed. Even Mr Bonkers was happy too – especially when he managed to sell (for a small fortune) the film he'd taken of Billy zooming across the water to one of the TV crews whose camera had failed to work. "Should have charged up the battery," Mr Bonkers advised them nonchalantly.

The following day, as Billy and his family sat down to a large – make that a VERY large – porridge breakfast, Mr Bonkers came back from the local shop with an armful of newspapers and spread them out on the table.

Every single one had a picture of Billy on the front page. "Miracle Boy! Wonder Kid! Child Sensation!" they all announced.

Billy Bonkers

Yes, for one day of his life, Billy had become the most famous person on the planet.

THE END

Billy Bonkers

and the
Ghost of Fatty Maclay

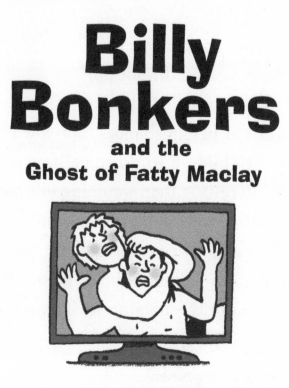

"You can't stay in and watch telly all day just because it's raining," said Mrs Bonkers to her family.

"Oh, come on, Mum," said Billy. "It's the wrestling."

"The only wrestling that I'm interested in around here," said Mrs Bonkers, "is wrestling with the wretched washing that this family never stops creating. Now, who can help me fold this lot up?"

Nobody moved. "Sausage," sighed Mrs Bonkers to her husband. "Can you please get your children to do something a little more interesting than watching oily men in swimsuits throw each other around."

"Uh, yes, of course, Piglet," said Mr Bonkers. "Dreadful rubbish. I don't know what the world is coming to. It's gone mad. The world's gone mad!"

"And now, folks…" announced a loud American voice from the television. "The man you've all been waiting for…our very own champion…Eddie 'Swamp Monster' MULLIGAN!"

"Nigel!"

You probably know by now that when Mrs Bonkers calls her husband by his real name it means that he must do exactly what she says, or there'll be trouble.

"Oh, um, yes, sorry, Piglet. Now children, come along, why don't we all go bowling?"

* * *

When the Bonkers family arrived at the bowling alley, a man had just finished putting up an extra sign above the alley's usual name, The Bowl-O-Drome.

Fatty Maclay's

the sign said.

"Oh," said Mr Bonkers. "Has there been a change of management?"

"No," said the man. "I'm still the manager, but I've decided to change the name in honour of the great Fatty Maclay. From now on, this is Fatty Maclay's Bowl-O-Drome."

"Who's Fatty Maclay?" asked Betty.

"Follow me," said the manager, leading the Bonkers family inside.

He pointed to an enormous framed picture of a very round, very red-faced man in a stripy shirt. The man had a big grin on his face. In one hand he held a bowling ball and in the other he had a large gold cup.

"That," said the manager, "is Fatty Maclay. He'd just scored the perfect 300; the maximum possible score. Look, that's the '300 Cup' in his hand. He did it in this very bowling alley...in that very lane." The manager pointed to a lane at the far end of the alley that was cordoned off with purple ropes. It was the only lane where no one was playing. The cup stood in a glass cabinet on the wall beside it.

"This photograph was taken the night before he disappeared – disappeared for ever!" sniffed the manager. "Oh, it was my fault! I should have been here. I should have been here to watch him but... boohoo...boo...hooo. Sniffle...sniffle."

"There, there," said Mrs Bonkers, giving the manager a reassuring pat on the back. "I'm sure it wasn't your fault."

"Disappeared?" said Billy. "How did he disappear?"

"Well, he'd come to do some practice," began the manager. "He practised here every night. I'd usually watch him. He was a local hero and he did so much for the club. But that night…" He sniffed and wiped his nose. "That fateful night, I went to my office to make a telephone call, and when I came back…he was gone. Gone! And he hasn't been seen since! I knew he hadn't just left because on the table beside his alley there was still half a plateful of cheesy chips. They were his favourite. He'd never leave before he'd finished his cheesy chips. Never!"

The manager broke down in tears again. "And every day," he squeaked, "every day I can hear his voice. It's as though his ghost is calling me…blaming me. 'HELP,' it wails.

H...E...L...P M...E!'"

"Well, um, look, I...uh...I
hate to interrupt," said
Mr Bonkers, coughing,
"but...um...any chance
of us having a game?"

"Oh, I'm so sorry,"
said the manager,
recovering himself
a little. "But we're
absolutely full today.
It's the rain, you know."

"Yes," said Mrs Bonkers. "That's why we're
here, too. Can't you just fit us in for one
little game? Please?"

"Oh, all right, then," said the manager.
"Seeing as you seem to be such a nice
family. I'll let you use that end lane: the
lane that was used by Fatty when he
disappeared. The ball-return system doesn't

work, though. The belt seems to be stuck, so you'll have to go and collect the balls yourselves every so often."

"No problem," said Mr Bonkers. "That's great. Thanks."

"First things first!" said Billy. "Cheesy chips! Please can we have cheesy chips, Dad?"

"It depends what your mother says," replied Mr Bonkers, looking at his wife. "Um, they're not very good for them, but…"

"Don't pretend to me that *you* don't love them as well," said Mrs Bonkers, smiling.

"OK, gang, cheesy chips for everyone. But only a small size...and no fizzy drinks!" she added.

So Betty, Billy and their dad sprinted to the snack bar, grabbed some cheesy chips and, in no time at all, they were getting ready at their lane in Fatty Maclay's Bowl-O-Drome.

Mr Bonkers typed everybody's names into the scoring computer. "Right then," he said. "All set up. I'll just go and get my 'bachelor balls' from the car."

"Oh no," said Betty. "Dad, you promised you'd give them away. They're so embarrassing."

Mr Bonkers returned to the lane and unzipped his carrying case.

"Sausage, I do think they're a bit inappropriate for a man of your age," said Mrs Bonkers, looking at her husband with a mixture of dismay and pity.

"Nonsense," replied Mr Bonkers, chirpily, as he picked a bowling ball from the case; a bowling ball decorated with an impossibly long American dragster racing car, with flames billowing from the exhaust and a painted snarling shark's mouth over the bonnet.

"Besides," he continued, "I couldn't possibly give them away. They're my *lucky* balls."

He took a huge run up, skidded to a halt at the top of the lane and blasted a ball down the alley. It piled along the edge of the lane before crashing into the side wall of the building, taking a bit of plaster off as it went.

"Hmm...just a rangefinder," he grunted. "It'll set me up for the next one." He hurled another ball down the alley, which rolled into the trench without hitting a single pin. "Slippery hands," he mumbled, rubbing his fingers together vigorously over the jet of air beside the rack of balls. "Go on, Piglet, your go."

Billy sat down to eat a few cheesy chips while his mum and sister took their turns. The chips were very floppy and greasy and the cheese was just like bright yellow warm goo. Billy LOVED them!

Cheesy Chips

Then he stood up and picked a ball. He
fitted his middle fingers inside
two of the holes and his
thumb inside the other.

He took a few steps backwards,
then strode forwards, swung his arm
like it was a pendulum and scooted
the ball down the lane.

"Woah!" shouted Billy, in surprise. His
fingers were so greasy from the chips that
the ball had accidentally slipped off them
at a very peculiar angle. It veered sideways,

spinning and skidding as it went, before straightening up, gathering speed and slamming full tilt right into the triangle of pins at the end of the alley, knocking them all over at once.

"Strike!" yelled Betty. "It's a strike!"

"Yes, I suppose it is!" said Billy. "My first ever!" He sat down to watch his family take their turns, feeling very pleased with himself indeed.

I think I'd better have a few more of those greasy chips, he thought.

Billy Bonkers

When it was his turn again, Billy picked up another bowling ball. Again, he strode down the approach, swung his arm, and let the ball slip off his fingers. The ball swerved away to the other side of the alley this time, then turned almost at right angles in the other direction. It hovered near the trench at the side of the alley for a few moments, before suddenly kicking back into the lane and flattening every single pin.

"You've done it again!" shouted Betty.

AMAZING!

"Wow!" said Billy, as astonished as he was the first time. "That was cool!"

Now, I don't know if you've ever been ten-pin bowling. But even if you have, it's quite hard to figure out how the scoring works, so I'll tell you. Every time you get a strike you get 10 points, or "pins" as they're called, PLUS the amount of pins that you knock down in your next 2 turns.

You get 10 turns in total and an extra 2 turns if you get a strike on your last turn. If this sounds a bit complicated – that's because it is. Let's just say that the most points you can ever get is 300. This is about as difficult as scoring a hole-in-one at golf, climbing Mount Everest on your own or a one-year-old baby being picked as captain of the England football team. It is very, very difficult indeed. And that, of course, is why Fatty Maclay was such a legend at the Bowl-O-Drome.

When Billy bowled his next ball, it seemed to slide out of the back of his hand. It shot off down the alley with a vicious backspin, which all but stopped the ball right in front of the pins. Then it curled in an almost perfect circle, taking down every pin with it as it went.

"That's a turkey!" yelled a man in the lane next to them. "Three strikes in a row! That's thirty points just for your first play! You're hot!"

As the game went on, to his complete amazement, Billy gathered more and more strikes. The ball was curling and swerving all over the place. It seemed to have a mind of its own. And, after every turn, Billy would sit down in astonishment and eat a few more cheesy chips.

Word of Billy's success had spread around the alley and it wasn't long before every other player in the Bowl-O-Drome had come over to watch this new young bowling genius at work.

At first it was a turkey, but then it was a four-bagger, a five-bagger, a six-bagger... every turn that Billy took would knock down all ten pins. He could not believe it, and nor could anyone else in the alley. His points went from 30 to 60 to 90 and on and on all the way up to 270.

A hush filled the Bowl-O-Drome. Billy was

only one bowl away from the perfect score: the magical 300. It would make him an all-time, world-famous bowling legend.

Billy reached for a ball, but there were none left.

"Here, son, use one of mine," said Mr Bonkers.

"Oh, Dad!" moaned Betty. But Billy was in the groove. He didn't want to break his concentration – or his run of luck – so, almost in a trance, he took his father's bowling ball.

Then Billy walked back to his table. "Just one more handful of cheesy chips," he said to himself. There was only one handful left. Billy lifted them to his lips.

A great, big dollop of sticky
yellow cheese hung from
them in gloopy strings. "Yum!"
said Billy, scooping it all
into his mouth. "Delicious!"

He stood a while in silence,
and took a deep breath to steady
his nerves. He slipped his two fingers
and his thumb into the holes on the ball.
They slid in easily. He gazed down the alley
at the ten pins, far in the distance, and held
the ball out in front of him.

I'll deliver this one really fast, he thought to
himself. *That way it'll all be over quickly. I'll
bowl it as hard as I can.*

It felt to Billy as though a thousand pairs
of eyes were watching him. Then he began
to stride down the approach towards the
delivery line. One step...two...three...he
lifted his arm backwards, held it for a

Whoooooosssshhhhh!!

moment, then swung it towards the triangle of pins with all his might. Then, as the whole crowd watched, Billy slipped, fell flat on his face and, before he knew what was happening, he felt himself hurtling down the alley, with the bowling ball stuck fast to his fingers!

Now, I don't know if you've ever eaten cheesy chips. Your parents are probably much too sensible to let you get anywhere near them. But, if you have, you'll know what I mean when I say that the cheese is very, very sticky indeed. In fact, it's hardly REAL cheese at all, is it? It's more like plastic. And, just as plastic melts into a gloopy liquid when it's hot, then gets stickier and harder as it cools down, so does that peculiar cheese. It comes out of the pump all runny and hot but, gradually, it becomes sticky and stringy and g u m m y and hard.

This is exactly what had happened to the cheese on Billy's chips. It had been getting colder and colder until it might as well have been squishy, yellow glue. And when Billy had slipped his cheesy fingers into his dad's bowling ball, they had stuck  fast to the sides of the three holes.

And that is why, right now, Billy was hurtling down the end lane of Fatty Maclay's Bowl-O-Drome at roughly a hundred miles an hour, with everybody watching him, and with his hand stuck tight to a bowling ball that had a picture of a shark-covered fire-belching American roadster on it.

This time, the ball (and Billy) slid down

the lane perfectly straight. It hit the front pin, then the next and the next. Pins went flying in all directions around Billy's face. As the ball flew on behind the pins, Billy just had time to look back and see that not a single pin was left standing.

Then, suddenly,
THUMP!
Billy had smashed
against the rubber
curtain at the end
of the alley. He
bounced back
from the curtain
into a chute and then
fell with a bump onto
what felt to him like a
kind of moving carpet.
Grrrrr...
went the carpet.
Then
ker-chunk!

ker-chunk!

Whirrrr!

"It's the ball-return system!" said the
manager. "Billy must have fallen onto it so
hard that he's bumped it back into action!"

Suddenly, an eerie sound filled the Bowl-O-Drome. "Aaah!" it went. Then "HELP! H...E...L...P M...E!"

"The ghost of Fatty Maclay!" shouted the manager, turning white with fear. "We've disturbed him! He's come back to haunt us!"

Meanwhile, Billy felt himself being dragged deep down into the bowels of the Bowl-O-Drome. It was so dark that he couldn't see a thing, but he was being carried along a very tight, narrow tunnel on what he now realised was a mini-conveyor belt – the kind that you see suitcases on at airports, but much,

much smaller. Every so often, he found himself completely wedged against the walls of the tunnel, and unable to move either forwards or backwards until a jolt from the belt pushed him along a little bit further.

Eventually his head hit a large, warm, squashy obstacle in the tunnel and he was able to move no further. Billy was completely stuck, but the conveyor belt was going **chuggety...chuggety...chuggety** underneath his trousers, scraping against his bottom until it was really very sore indeed.

"Stop the machine!" yelled Mrs Bonkers. "Stop it now or it'll chop our Billy into mincemeat. He'll be nothing but little sausages, squishing one after another, *plop, plop, plop,* out of this terrible machine!"

"Be quiet, Piglet," shouted Mr Bonkers. "Honestly, you're making so much noise that I can't even hear myself think!"

"Little Billy sausages…" wailed Mrs Bonkers again.

"Hang on a minute," said Betty, who had silently been watching this whole episode. "I think I might have an idea! We shouldn't try to *stop* the machine. What we should do is make it go *faster*…as fast as it possibly can!"

"Faster?" said Mrs Bonkers. "Betty, are you out of your mind?"

"No," said Betty. "Listen, if you push a piece of cork very tightly into the end of a popgun, you have to fire it really, really hard in order to release the cork. The pressure builds and builds inside the gun until…

BANG! the cork finally comes shooting out as fast as a bullet from the end of the barrel."

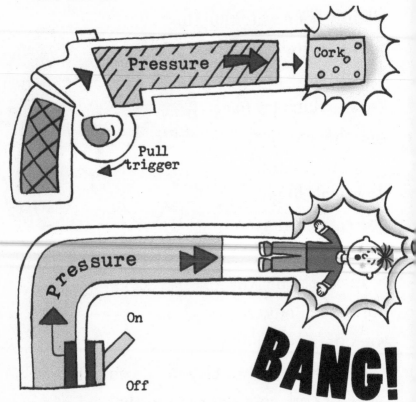

"Lordy lorks!" cried Mrs Bonkers. "She's finally lost it. Loopy as a fruit cake. Nutty as nougat!"

"Look," said Betty. "Don't you see? Billy's the cork and the ball-return system is, well...that's the gun. If we make the belt go fast enough, we should be able to fire Billy right out of...wherever it is that he's got stuck."

"Betty," said Mr Bonkers. "You may be crazy, but it might just be worth a try."

So the manager went to his control panel and turned the belt on the ball-return system in the Bonkers' bowling lane right up to full speed.

Chuggety...chuggety...chuggety

Billy felt the belt whirring faster and faster. It was pushing him harder and harder against the huge obstruction in front of him. Every movement of the belt

was squishing him
tighter until he
felt as though
he could stand
it no longer.
Something
had to give.
And, luckily, it did.

BANG! I've never seen an elephant
shot out of a drinking straw. But, if I had,
I imagine it would look a bit like what the
assembled crowd at Fatty Maclay's Bowl-O-
Drome now saw. To everyone's complete
and utter astonishment, from the
mouth of the ball-return system
right next to the lane that Billy
and his family had been
bowling in, shot a very round,
very red-faced figure in a
stripy bowling shirt.

"It's Fatty!" gasped the manager. "It's Fatty Maclay himself!" He gave a strange kind of yelp and then immediately fainted on the floor.

And he was right – like a cork from a popgun (or an elephant from a drinking straw), Fatty Maclay hurtled out of the ball-return system, closely followed by a very startled-looking, very bruised, Billy.

Billy Bonkers

They flew through the air together, over the incredulous heads of all the other people in the alley until, finally, they fell with a

osh!

(well, two sploshes, in fact) into the huge
vat of cheese sauce that was bubbling away
in the snack bar next to the chips.

"Lordy lorks, you're alive!" cried Mrs Bonkers, as Billy surfaced. Then, "Oh, my goodness, look at you! Think of the washing!"

"It's you! It's really you!" yelled the manager, who had now recovered and was running as fast as he could towards Fatty Maclay.

"Yes," said Fatty Maclay, licking the cheese from his lips. "I've been stuck in there for days and, finally, this brave boy has rescued me!" He put his arm around Billy's shoulders and smiled.

"I've been shouting and shouting for help but nobody came to find me."

"What *happened* to you?" said the manager. "We didn't know where you'd gone. You just disappeared!"

"Well, there I was, just practising on my own that night," began Fatty Maclay, "when my ball got stuck at the end of the lane. I went down to get it and I just tripped. The next thing I knew, I'd rolled down a chute and fallen onto the ball-return conveyor belt. I couldn't get up and, before long, I was wedged tight inside the tunnel. I couldn't move forwards or backwards. So there I stayed until, finally, this chap came and pushed me out.

"I could have died down there," he added. "This boy's a hero. A total hero!" Then he turned to Billy. "What's your name?" he asked.

"Bonkers," replied Billy. "Billy Bonkers."

"Well, Billy Bonkers," said Fatty Maclay, "are you any good at bowling?"

"Good?" said Mr Bonkers. "He's amazing! He's just equalled your record. Look!"

Fatty Maclay looked up at the scoring computer. 300, it said.

"Unbelievable!" said Fatty Maclay. "Congratulations!" Then he spotted the bowling ball that was still stuck to the ends of Billy's fingers. "Hey, nice ball!" he said. "What a car! That is *COOL!*"

"Have it!" said Betty quickly. "Please, have them all!" she grabbed the rest of her dad's balls and held them out to Fatty.

The Ghost of Fatty Maclay

"Really?" said Fatty Maclay, his eyes lighting up as though they were the most extraordinary treasures he had ever seen. "Can I?"

"Yes!" said Billy, Betty and their mother all at once. Even Mr Bonkers nodded sheepishly.

"Then *you*, my friend," said Fatty Maclay, reaching into the glass cabinet on the wall beside the lane, "*you* must have this." He carefully lifted out the cup: the huge, gold "300 Cup".

"Wow!" said Billy. "Thank you!"

"Hang on a minute," said Fatty. "I'm absolutely starving, and I've just realised why! I've been stuck inside that tunnel and I haven't eaten anything for days. Chips all round! Cheesy chips for everyone...

ICE CREA

Cheesy Chips

...and fizzy drinks...and hot dogs...and doughnuts...and ice cream! Let's party! Let's make this a day to remember!"

And, as Billy went home with his family that night, still covered in cheese and clutching the huge "300 Cup" in his arms, he knew that it was a day he would *never* forget. Not even if he lived to be a hundred and twenty-three.

THE END

More Orchard books you might enjoy

Billy Bonkers
Giles Andreae & Nick Sharratt   978 1 84616 151 3   £4.99

Beast Quest: Ferno the Fire Dragon
Adam Blade   978 1 84616 483 5   £4.99

Beast Quest: Sepron the Sea Serpent
Adam Blade   978 1 84616 482 8   £4.99

Beast Quest: Arcta the Mountain Giant
Adam Blade   978 1 84616 484 2   £4.99

Beast Quest: Tagus the Horse-Man
Adam Blade   978 1 84616 486 6   £4.99

Beast Quest: Nanook the Snow Monster
Adam Blade   978 1 84616485 9   £4.99

Beast Quest: Epos the Flame Bird
Adam Blade   978 1 84616 487 3   £4.99

The Fire Within
Chris d'Lacey   978 1 84121 533 4   £5.99

Icefire
Chris d'Lacey   978 1 84362 134 8   £5.99

Fire Star
Chris d'Lacey   978 1 84362 522 3   £5.99

The Fire Eternal
Chris d'Lacey   978 1 84616 426 2   £5.99

Orchard books are available from all good bookshops, or can be ordered direct
from the publisher: Orchard Books, PO BOX 29, Douglas IM99 1BQ
Credit card orders please telephone 01624 836000 or fax 01624 837033 or visit our website:
www.orchardbooks.co.uk or email: bookshop@enterprise.net for details.

To order please quote title, author and ISBN and your full name and address.
Cheques and postal orders should be made payable to 'Bookpost plc.'
Postage and packing is FREE within the UK (overseas customers should add £1.00 per book).

Prices and availability are subject to change.